Emma's Vacation

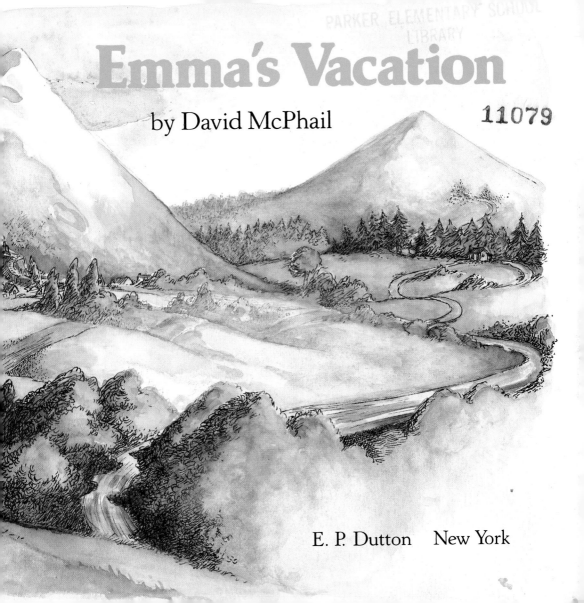

Emma's Vacation

by David McPhail

E. P. Dutton   New York

The author wishes to thank
John O'Connor for his help.

Copyright © 1987 by David McPhail
All rights reserved.

Library of Congress Cataloging in Publication Data
McPhail, David M.
 Emma's vacation.
 Summary: Emma's idea of a good vacation is
quite different from that of her parents.
 [1. Vacations—Fiction] I. Title.
PZ7.M2427Eo 1987 [E] 86-24066
ISBN 0-525-44315-0

Published in the United States by E. P. Dutton,
2 Park Avenue, New York, N.Y. 10016

Published simultaneously in Canada by
Fitzhenry & Whiteside Limited, Toronto

Editor: Ann Durell

Printed in Hong Kong by South China Printing Co.
First Edition   COBE   10 9 8 7 6 5 4 3 2 1

Emma and her mother and father were
going on vacation.

It was a long ride.

Getting lost made the ride even longer.

When they finally got there, it was raining.

The roof of the cabin leaked in some places.

In the morning, the sun was shining.
Emma wanted to climb a mountain.

"We'll drive," said her father.

They went out to lunch.

They rode on a boat and a bus...

and a train

and a rocket ship.

The next day, Emma wouldn't budge.
"I want to stay here," she said.

"Here?" said her mother and father.
"What can we do here?"

"We can wade in the brook," said Emma,

"and try to catch a fish."

"We can pick some berries

and climb a tree."

"We can pack a picnic and go for a hike.

When we get back, we can lie in the
hammock and sing songs and tell stories."

Emma was having a wonderful vacation.